# Dante's Peak

a novelization by
DEWEY GRAM
based on the motion picture
written by LESLIE BOHEM

Level 2

Retold by Robin Waterfield
Series Editors: Andy Hopkins and Jocelyn Potter

**Pearson Education Limited**
Edinburgh Gate, Harlow,
Essex CM20 2JE, England
and Associated Companies throughout the world.

ISBN: 978-1-4058-6973-7

First published in the USA by Boulevard Books, by arrangement with
MCA Publishing Rights, a Division of MCA, Inc. 1997
First published in Great Britain by Puffin Books 1997
This adaptation first published by Penguin Books Ltd 1998
Published by Addison Wesley Longman Ltd and Penguin Books Ltd 1998
New edition first published 1999
This edition first published 2008

3  5  7  9  10  8  6  4  2

Copyright © MCA Publishing Rights, a Division of MCA, Inc. 1997
Illustrations copyright © Chris Brown 1998
Text copyright © Penguin Books Ltd 1999
This edition copyright © Pearson Education Ltd 2008

Typeset by Graphicraft Ltd, Hong Kong
Set in 11/14pt Bembo
Printed in China
SWTC/02

Published by Pearson Education Ltd in association with
Penguin Books Ltd, both companies being subsidiaries of Pearson Plc

For a comp ... ite to your local
Pearson I ... on Education,

# *Contents*

# Introduction

*'Listen, Paul,' Harry said. 'We have a problem. That volcano's getting ready to explode.'*

*Dreyfus stopped smiling. 'I know it was hard for you up there, Harry,' he said, 'but you mustn't get excited. Nothing much happened.'*

*'Nothing much happened?' said Harry. 'Paul, I was there. That was a big earthquake.'*

Harry Dalton, a scientist, knows a lot about earthquakes and volcanoes. He works at the United States Volcano Office. His boss, Paul Dreyfus, sends him to the small town of Dante's Peak in the northwest of the US. The town is on a mountain, and the mountain is moving.

Harry thinks that the old volcano above the town is going to explode. But Paul thinks Harry is wrong. The town's mayor, Rachel Wando, and businessmen have big plans for Dante's Peak. They don't want to hear about dangerous volcanoes.

But is Harry wrong? How many people must die before they know he is right? When the mountain explodes, can Harry help Rachel and her children?

The volcano in the story is near a real volcano in the US. This real volcano is Mount St Helens, and it exploded in 1980. It was the US's biggest volcanic explosion: it killed many people and took out 250 homes, 47 bridges and 300 kilometres of road.

*Dante's Peak* first came to cinemas in America seventeen years later in 1997. In the film, Pierce Brosnan plays Harry Dalton and Linda Hamilton is Rachel Wando. Leslie Bohem wrote the story for the film, and Roger Donaldson made the film. Then Dewey Gram wrote the book of the film.

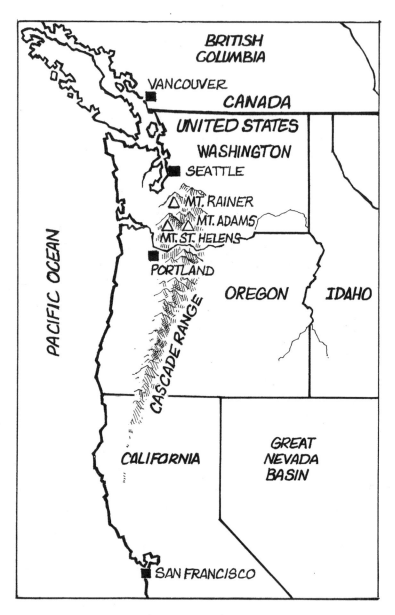

*The west United States.*

# Chapter 1   A Dangerous Job

Harry Dalton loved volcanoes. He had the most dangerous and exciting job in the world. He was a scientist, and he wanted to understand volcanoes. 'Volcanoes kill people,' he said. 'When we understand volcanoes, we can tell people: "This mountain is going to explode", and then they can move away.' He flew round the world. Was a volcano ready to explode? Harry Dalton was there.

His girlfriend Marianne loved volcanoes too. Then one day in South America they stayed too long near an exploding volcano. The mountain sent rock and ash up into the sky. A small rock came down on to their car, hit Marianne, and she died.

Harry was never the same again. He worked harder – too hard. He wanted to understand everything about volcanoes before a volcano killed anybody again. Marianne was dead: no others must die.

Some months later, his boss, Paul Dreyfus, called him into his office. 'Harry,' he said, 'you must take a holiday. You're tired. You're not twenty now, you're thirty-six. I'm sorry about Marianne, but volcanoes are going to explode. You can't stop them.'

Harry took a holiday. He went round the world – but there are volcanoes all round the world. So he always found work. After a year, he came back to the office. His friends – Terry Furlong, Stan Tzima, Nancy Field and Greg Esmail – all smiled when Harry came back. 'We knew it,' they said. 'You love your work. "Harry will come back soon", we said. And here you are.'

♦

'Harry,' said Paul Dreyfus two or three days later, 'something is happening up in the Cascades. Our equipment shows that one of

1

the mountains there is moving, but not much. Nobody there knows it, but our equipment is good.'

'In the Cascades?' Harry said. 'Here in the United States . . . in Washington?'

'That's right. Dante's Peak, near Mount Washington. We all remember 1980 when Mount St Helen's exploded. Can you go?'

'I'm leaving now,' said Harry.

He put some equipment in the back of his off-road car, and drove to Washington. There were tall trees thick on the mountains. 'It's very beautiful here.' Harry thought. He saw the morning sun on mountain lakes to the left of the road.

The mountain stood tall over the small town of Dante's Peak. Only seven thousand people lived there. It was quiet.

Harry drove to the centre of the town and found the hotel. Mr Cluster showed him to his room. Then Harry asked, 'Where's Mayor Wando? Do you know?'

'Yeah,' said Cluster. 'She's speaking to the people of the town today at the school. A newspaper called Dante's Peak "The Second Best Town in America" and they're giving the newspaper photograph of the town to the people.'


## Chapter 2   The Best Town in America

'I'm going to be late,' Rachel Wando said. She ran round her room at home. 'Where's my other shoe?' she said.

'You're always late, Mom,' said Lauren, Rachel's ten-year-old daughter. Rachel was thirty-five. 'And your shoe is under the bed.'

'What am I going to say?' Rachel said. ' "I want to say thank you to Karen from the newspaper. She came here . . ." ' Rachel stopped. 'Is it Karen or Kathy from the newspaper?' she asked.

'For the tenth time, Mom,' said Lauren, 'she's Karen.'

*'I'm going to be late,' Rachel Wando said.*

'Where's my good jacket.'

'You don't have a good jacket.'

'The blue jacket.'

'It's on the back of the chair down in the kitchen.'

Rachel ran down to the kitchen. She put on her jacket and then called through the door of her son's bedroom: 'Graham, let's go!'

'He's not in,' said Lauren. 'He'll meet us there. He told me. Come on!'

♦

Harry stood quietly in a corner of the room. Most of the people from the town were there. Les Worrell, the most important businessman in the town, sat with Karen Narlington from the newspaper. He looked at the chair next to him. Where was that woman?

Rachel ran into the room and then slowed to a walk. Les stood up and said, 'And here's the mayor, Rachel Wando.'

Harry watched Rachel. 'Wow!' he thought. 'The mayor is a woman . . . and she's beautiful!'

Rachel came up to the front of the room, smiled at Les and Karen, and sat down in her chair. First Karen spoke. Then Rachel stood up, and said: 'I want to say thank you to Kathy from the newspaper . . .'

'It's Karen,' Lauren called from the back of the room. Everybody laughed.

Rachel smiled. 'We like our town. Now Karen's newspaper likes it too. And people read her newspaper all round America. This is important for the town of Dante's Peak. So we thank you, Karen. She thinks that Dante's Peak is the second best town in America. We know better. It's the *first*, the best place to live. And next year, with the help of Elliot Blair, we'll show America. Karen's newspaper will say: "Dante's Peak — the best town in all America."'

She stopped talking and sat down. The people in the room jumped to their feet, with smiles on their faces. Harry turned to the man next to him. 'Who's Elliot Blair?' he asked.

'He's a big businessman,' the man said. 'He wants to bring a lot of money to Dante's Peak. He wants to make the town a centre for people's winter holidays. There'll be a lot of work for people here.'

## Chapter 3   Two Swimmers

Behind the town, up in the mountain, was a famous warm lake. Swimmers often went there. That day, two visitors, a young man and a young woman, walked up to the lake for a swim. The trees were green, the sun was in the sky. It was quiet and beautiful.

The woman put her foot in the water. 'Ow!' she said. 'It's hot!'

'Yes,' said her friend, 'I know. The lake is famous.'

They laughed, and walked into the water. They played and swam. 'This is good,' said the young woman. 'Do you want to come and live here?'

'No, it's too quiet,' said the man. 'Nothing exciting happens.'

Suddenly birds flew up from the trees, and they heard the sound of animals. 'Why are the animals running away?' she asked.

'I don't know,' he answered. He pulled her under the water, and she laughed.

Suddenly, there was a small earthquake. Now the woman was afraid. She swam over to the man. Under the lake rocks moved and the ground opened. Hot gas exploded into the lake. She screamed. 'The water!' she cried. 'It's too hot! It's . . .' They were her last words.

Soon the lake was quiet again.

◆

From the school, Rachel went to find her daughter. A tall, dark-eyed man walked up to her and said, 'Hi! I'm Harry Dalton, from the United States Volcano Office, and . . .'

But Les Worrell and Elliot Blair came up to Rachel with smiles on their faces. 'Well done, Rachel!' Les said, before Harry could say anything more.

'You're a good speaker,' Blair said.

'Thank you,' Rachel said. But she didn't want Dalton and Blair to meet. Blair wanted to make Dante's Peak a holiday town, Dalton was from the Volcano Office. No, she didn't want them to meet.

Harry tried again. 'I'm Harry Dalton, from . . .'

'From Portland,' Rachel said quickly. 'Yes, your boss spoke to me on the phone. He asked me to show you round. Let's go.'

She took him by the arm and moved him away from Worrell and Blair. Lauren came up to them. 'Where's your brother?' Rachel asked.

'I don't know,' Lauren said.

'I think I do,' Rachel said. They went over to her car. 'Get in,' Rachel said to Harry. 'I must find my thirteen-year-old son first.'

They took the road up the mountain. Rachel told Harry about Blair. 'He's going to be very good for the town,' she said.

'Where are we going?' Harry asked. He wanted to start work.

Rachel stopped the car outside an old mine. She got out of the car and went over to it. 'Graham!' she called. 'Graham, are you in there?'

A minute later, three boys came out of the mine. They were dirty. 'You two go home,' Rachel said angrily to the other two boys. 'And you – get in the car!'

Graham looked at Harry. 'Who are you?' he asked.

'I'm . . .' Harry began, but Rachel said: 'That mine is dangerous. Rocks can fall. You mustn't go in there. How many times do I have to tell you?'

'Mom, not now, OK?' Graham said. He looked at Harry. Harry smiled at him.

*A minute later, three boys came out of the mine.*

## Chapter 4   Dead Fish on the Water

They drove up the mountain. 'Hey, Mom,' said Graham. 'Why don't you leave me at Ruth's?'

'Yeah, me too,' said Lauren.

'There's no time,' Rachel said. 'Mr Dalton wants to start working now.'

'Oh, please, Mom,' said the children.

'It's OK with me,' said Harry.

'Ruth is my husband's mother,' Rachel said, 'but my husband left me.'

Ruth lived by a cold, clean mountain lake. They drove up to her small house. A dog ran out of the house and jumped up at the car.

'Hi, Roughy!' Lauren said through the window.

They all got out of the car. Graham took an old shoe and threw it for Roughy. The dog ran into the trees after it.

Lauren ran over to the house. 'Hello, where are you?' she called.

An older woman came out of the house with a big smile on her face. She wore a shirt and jeans. 'Hi!' she said. The children ran over to her, but Rachel walked slowly. 'Hello, Ruth,' she said.

Ruth looked at Harry. 'Is this your boyfriend?' she asked.

Harry answered. 'No,' he said. 'I'm from the United States Volcano Office. I want to look at your mountain.'

'Yeah, people came here in 1980, after Mount St Helen's,' said Ruth. 'There wasn't a problem with this mountain then, and there isn't now.'

Harry looked round at the lake. There were brown, dead trees by the water. 'When did those trees die?' he asked.

'Trees are always dying,' Ruth said. 'Then new trees come. We had a bad winter.'

*They all got out of the car. Graham took an old shoe
and threw it for Roughy.*

Harry took some equipment out of his bag and went over to the lake. Graham followed him. 'What are you doing?' he asked.

Harry said: 'This equipment will answer the question: How much acid is there in the lake?' He looked at the equipment. There was too much acid. He put his finger into the water. Not good. He went back to the car.

'I'm going to take Mr Dalton up to the warm lake,' Rachel said to Ruth. 'Can the children stay here?'

'Yes, but why don't we all go?' said Ruth.

'Yeah,' said Graham. 'We can go for a swim.'

The children ran over to the car. Rachel looked angrily at Ruth. Harry smiled. 'These two women don't like being together,' he thought.

♦

In the car, Rachel asked about the acid in the water. 'It's not good,' Harry said.

'Do we have a problem?' she asked. 'Will the mountain explode?'

'I don't know,' he answered. 'Often nothing happens. People hear sounds under the ground, there are earthquakes, trees die, there's acid in the water – and then nothing happens.'

Rachel stopped the car near the warm lake. The children jumped out of the car. 'Come on!' they cried. 'Let's go!'

'Wait for me!' Rachel called.

'Oh, they'll be OK,' Ruth said. She followed the children.

Harry started getting equipment out of the car. Suddenly Lauren screamed. Rachel ran through the trees. Harry followed.

'Look!' Lauren cried. On the ground at her feet were two dead animals.

'There are a lot of those round here this year,' Ruth said. 'Do you think they're ill?'

The children went over to the lake. Graham stood on a rock.

He wanted to jump in. Suddenly Harry called, 'Stop!' There was a lot of gas. 'There are some dead fish on the water,' he said, 'and there's something bigger too. What is it?'

Children can see things better. Lauren screamed again. 'A man and a woman. There, face down, in the water!'

## Chapter 5  Sleeping, not Dead

Some men from the hospital carried the swimmers away. Harry was on the phone to Paul Dreyfus. 'Yes, there is a problem here,' he said. 'Send everyone – and the robot.'

He listened to Paul's answer. 'Yes, I know about the money,' he said, 'but we're talking about people here. Two people are dead.' He put his phone away.

'Are you OK?' he asked the children.

'Yes,' they said.

'Who were those swimmers?' Harry asked. 'Do you know?'

'They weren't from the town,' Rachel said. 'I think they were visitors. Do we have a big problem here, Harry?'

'I don't know. I must talk to the most important people in the town.'

'OK,' Rachel said. 'I'm the mayor. I'll tell them you want to meet them.'

They met that evening. Eight people were in the room – Harry, Rachel, Les Worrell, and five other men and women from the town. Harry and Rachel told the others about the swimmers and the acid in the lake.

'But this volcano is dead,' said Sheriff Turner. 'The last explosion was seven thousand years ago.'

'No, it's sleeping, not dead,' Harry said. 'And I think it's starting to be dangerous again now.'

'Mr Dalton,' Les Worrell said, 'you want to move over seven

*Harry was on the phone to Paul Dreyfus. 'Yes, there is a problem here,' he said.*

thousand people from their homes. They aren't going to like that.'

'That's right,' said two or three of the others.

'Do you want people to die?' Harry asked.

'Do you *know* that people will die?' Les said.

'No, I don't know. But I want people to be ready to move out.'

'And what about Elliot Blair?' Les said. 'What will we say when he asks, "Why are people leaving? Is there a problem with the town?" Mr Dalton, do you think that he'll put money into the town after that?'

Everybody in the room started talking at the same time. Suddenly, Paul Dreyfus walked into the room.

'Paul!' said Harry. 'You're here. Did you bring . . . ?'

'Yes,' Paul said, 'I brought everything. We're staying at the hotel and our office will be there. Now, what's happening here?'

'Everybody,' called Harry, 'this is my boss, Paul Dreyfus. Paul, I want the people in the town to be ready to leave. We're talking about it now.'

Paul looked at the others. He said, 'Harry come with me.'

He took Harry outside. 'This isn't right,' he said. 'You're a scientist. You don't *know* that the volcano will explode.'

'Two people are dead,' Harry said. 'How many more people must die?'

'There's some acid in the water, there are some dead trees and animals. Why do you think "Volcano!"? There are earthquakes, and you get acid in the water. You know that. I think that there was one earthquake, and that's all. I don't think the volcano is going to explode.'

'But, Paul . . .'

'No,' Paul said. 'I'm the boss. I think you're wrong.'

He turned and went back into the room. When Harry was there too, Paul said, 'Everybody, Harry Dalton is a good man. He only wanted to help, but I don't think the volcano will explode. Don't say anything to other people in the town. We don't want them to be afraid. The other scientists and I will stay here for a week or two. We'll take our equipment up into the mountain. When we know anything, I'll tell you. But I don't think we'll find any danger.'

The businessmen were very happy. Then they turned angrily to Rachel. 'That was a mistake, Rachel,' they said. 'Why did you get us all in here? We don't want Blair to hear about it.'

Rachel looked at Dreyfus and Harry. Which of them was right?


## Chapter 6   The Mountain Waits


Dreyfus and Harry walked over to Stein's Bar. 'I want you out of here,' Dreyfus said. 'Take a holiday . . . now! Goodbye. I'll see you in two weeks.'

'No,' said Harry. 'I won't go. I'm your best man, and this town has problems.'

'Yes,' said Paul, 'you *are* my best man. But you must understand something. After we go, the people here in Dante's Peak will stay. They have their shops and their businesses. You think only about volcanoes, but this is about money too.'

'OK,' Harry said with a smile. 'I understand.'

'OK,' said Paul. 'Tomorrow we'll get a helicopter. I want you to fly round the peak with your equipment. What's happening? Why? You find the answers, and then you come and tell me.'

'Right,' Harry said, 'I'll do that.' Then he turned away and had a drink with Terry Furlong and the others.

The next morning Harry went into the Blue Moon Café for breakfast. This was Rachel's café.

She smiled at him. 'Coffee?' she asked.

'Yes, please,' he said. 'I'm sorry about yesterday. I only wanted to help. I'm better with volcanoes than I am with business people.'

'I know you wanted to help.' Rachel put the coffee back on the warmer, turned and said: 'Do you want to come to dinner tonight? I want to say thank you.'

'Thank you? What for?'

'You stopped Graham jumping into that water.'

'OK. Yes, please. I *do* want to have dinner with you.'

Later in the morning, Harry and Terry went out in the helicopter. They took a lot of equipment and flew round the peak. Terry watched the equipment. 'There's some gas,' he said. 'But not a lot.'

They couldn't see under the helicopter, so they didn't see it: the ground suddenly gave a strong push. Big rocks fell down the mountain. Then everything was quiet again. The mountain waited.

♦

*Later in the morning, Harry and Terry went out in the helicopter.*

After dinner that evening at Rachel's house, Harry and Rachel sat outside. They looked at the lights of the town.

'I know it's a little town,' she said. 'I know it's not important. But I love it here. It's my home.'

'Were you born here?' Harry asked.

'Yes.'

'And . . . um . . . you lived with your husband here?'

'Yes.' She was quiet for a moment. 'Brian and I were too young when we met. That was the problem. He left about six years ago. He never writes or anything. The children don't remember him. I don't think he writes to Ruth.'

'But you're OK,' he said.

'Yeah, I am . . . now. What about you? No wife?'

'No. I move round the world all the time. There was somebody at one time, but . . .' He told her about Marianne.

'I'm sorry,' Rachel said.

'Volcanoes are dangerous,' said Harry. 'People must know that.'

'Perhaps you're wrong about our volcano,' said Rachel. 'But I'm happy that you're here to help.'

## Chapter 7   Terry's Robot

The next day Harry, Stan and Terry went up the mountain. They left equipment here and there, near the peak. 'Now we'll know when the ground moves,' Stan said. 'We can see it on our equipment in the office at the hotel.'

'Yeah,' said Terry, 'when a bird jumps on to the ground, we'll know it. How was dinner last night, Harry?'

Harry didn't say anything.

'For a mayor, she's very beautiful,' said Terry.

Harry didn't say anything. Terry smiled.

Terry Furlong built robots. 'We can't get inside volcanoes,' he

*Terry went over to the robot and kicked it. The robot started again.*

said, 'but my little robots can. They can see for us, find gases and smoke for us. How hot is it? How dangerous is it? My robots can tell us. We can sit in the office, turn on our equipment, and see with the robot's eyes.'

Two days later, they put Terry's robot in the car park and turned it on. It walked for a few metres. 'Yeah, come on, robot!' called Terry. The robot stopped.

'Is there a problem?' asked Paul.

'No,' said Terry. He went over to the robot and kicked it. The robot started again. 'It will be OK on the peak,' said Terry.

They went to Rachel's café for coffee. She knew them all well now. 'One black coffee,' she said, 'two with only milk, and two with sugar too.'

She gave them their coffees. Then she asked, 'What's happening? What are you finding?'

'Our equipment shows that every day there are between twenty-five and seventy-five earthquakes,' Nancy said.

*Ten metres above Terry, a large rock broke away and fell on Terry and the robot.*

'What?' cried Rachel.

Harry laughed. 'It's OK,' he said. 'Nothing dangerous is happening. There are always small earthquakes. We can see them with our equipment, but they're not dangerous.'

The next day Terry and Harry took the robot to the peak and sent it inside the old volcano. The robot's 'eyes' sent pictures back to their equipment, and back to the equipment in the hotel too.

The robot walked on. Suddenly it stopped. 'Oh, no!' said Terry. He started to go after it.

'Be careful!' Harry said.

Terry climbed down into the old volcano. He put his feet down carefully on the ground. Good! It was hard. He walked on.

Back at the hotel, everybody watched the robot's pictures. They didn't look at their other equipment.

Terry found the robot and kicked it. The robot started moving again. 'OK, Terry, come back now,' Harry said on his radio.

Terry didn't listen. He followed the robot down inside the mountain.

Back in the hotel, Nancy stood up. She turned round. 'Oh, no!' she said. 'Look at this equipment!'

The others turned round. 'A strong earthquake is happening,' she said.

Paul called Harry on the radio. 'Come back now,' he said.

'What did you say?' asked Harry. 'I couldn't hear you.'

'I said, "Come back now," ' Paul said. 'Earthquake!'

But it was too late. Ten metres above Terry, a large rock broke away and fell on Terry and the robot.

Harry screamed into his radio: 'Terry! Terry!' But no answer came.

The rocks broke two of the robot's 'eyes'. Back in the hotel they couldn't see very well. Paul said, 'Harry, what's happening?'

'Get that helicopter up here now!' Harry said.

He started to climb down into the volcano. Some more rocks

fell near him. There were rocks all round, but where was Terry? Then he saw the colours of Terry's shirt. He pulled some rocks away. Terry looked up at him and smiled.

'There's something wrong with my leg,' he said.

Harry looked. 'The rocks broke Terry's leg,' he said into the radio. 'Tell the helicopter man, Hutcherson, to bring some help.'

Before long, Harry could hear the helicopter. He spoke to Hutcherson on the radio.

'Nearer! Nearer!' he called.

But now there was smoke coming out of the old volcano. Hutcherson was afraid. 'I'm not coming any nearer than that!' he said.

'You must!' Harry said. 'Only fifteen more metres! Down! Down!'

Slowly the helicopter came nearer. It pulled Terry and Harry inside and flew off down the mountain.

## Chapter 8  Bad for Business

The helicopter came down near the town. 'Look,' Terry said to Harry. 'A lot of people are waiting for us. We're famous!'

Harry smiled but said nothing. Doctors took Terry to hospital. Rachel pushed through the people and came up to Harry. 'Are you OK?' she said.

'Yeah, I'm OK,' he said.

Paul Dreyfus drove up in his car. 'I must go and talk to Paul,' Harry said to Rachel.

'How's Terry?' Paul asked.

'He'll be OK,' Harry said. 'But listen, Paul. We have a problem. That volcano's getting ready to explode.'

Dreyfus stopped smiling. 'I know it was hard for you up there,

20

*Hutcherson was afraid. 'I'm not coming any nearer than that!' he said.*

Harry,' he said, 'but you mustn't get excited. Not a lot happened.'

'Not a lot happened?' said Harry. 'Paul, I was there. That was a big earthquake.'

'But the mountain didn't explode,' Paul said. 'Terry was unlucky, that's all. Those rocks were weak.'

'No, Paul, listen,' Harry said. 'I think the lava is moving up nearer to the ground. The ground is too warm up there.'

'No, you listen, Harry,' said Paul angrily. 'You lost Marianne. Now you're always afraid. Well, I'm sorry about Marianne, but I don't want people in Dante's Peak to be afraid because you lost her.'

The two men started to fight, but Greg pulled Harry away. 'Careful, Harry,' he said.

Dreyfus walked away. 'Two more days,' he told them. 'We'll stay only two more days. There's nothing more for us to do here.'

♦

Three days later, they were ready to leave. In the evening, Harry went to Stein's Bar. Terry was back from the hospital. He was in the bar with Nancy, Greg and Stan. Harry met Rachel there, and they went to a quiet table in a corner with their drinks.

'Perhaps you'll come down to Portland one day, and we'll meet again,' he said.

'I usually have a lot of things to do,' said Rachel.

'Don't you take holidays?' he asked.

'Holidays? Oh, yes, I remember holidays. You have holidays when you don't have two children and a café, and aren't mayor of a town.'

Paul Dreyfus came over to their table. 'Can I sit down?' he said.

'Yes,' they answered.

'Before we leave,' Paul said to Rachel, 'I want to say thank you, Mayor Wando. You'll be happy to see us go.'

'Yes,' said Harry. He looked at Elliot Blair and Les Worrell. They sat together at a table. 'Our visit here was bad for business, I think.'

Worrell and Blair came over too. Les said, 'I told Mr Blair, "Look, the volcano people are leaving. There can't be any danger here." Am I right?'

Elliot Blair said, 'Yeah. I want to put eighteen million dollars into Dante's Peak, not Pompeii.'★

Paul laughed. 'No, there's no danger.' Then he turned to Harry. 'You're a scientist, Harry. Can you say that it's dangerous here?'

Dreyfus waited. Blair and Worrell looked at Harry. Then Harry said, 'No, I can't.'

Dreyfus smiled. 'Come over to the bar,' he said to Blair and Worrell. 'I'll buy you two a drink.'

A minute later Rachel said, 'It's getting late. I must go home to the children.'

'I'll walk with you,' Harry said. They got up and left.

The lake near Ruth's home was quiet and dark. But under the ground a lot of acid flowed into it. Fish died. First one fish, then ten, twenty, a hundred . . .

## Chapter 9   Dark Smoke

It was a beautiful night. Rachel and Harry walked down the street through the centre of town.

'What time are you going tomorrow?' she asked.

'Six o'clock in the morning,' he said.

'I'm sorry you're leaving,' she said.

---

★ Pompeii was a town in Italy. In A.D. 79 Mount Vesuvius, a volcano, exploded and the lava and ash finished the town.

*He put his arms round her. Then a car drove down the street.*

'It's OK,' he said. 'Our equipment is here. We can sit in Portland and answer the question: "What's happening in Dante's Peak?" No problem.'

'I know,' she said. 'But I'm sorry *you* have to go.'

Harry turned to Rachel, and she turned to him. He put his arms round her. Then a car drove down the street. The driver slowed the car near them. 'Good evening, Rachel,' a woman said. Then she drove away.

'Jeannie Lane,' Rachel said. 'She'll talk about this for the next two weeks.'

They walked to her house. When they were there she said, 'Do you want to come in for coffee or something?'

'Yes,' he said.

Inside, she fell into his arms, but suddenly Lauren called from her bedroom. 'Mommy, is that you? I'm thirsty.'

'I'll bring you a glass of water,' Rachel said.

She went into the kitchen. 'Oh, look,' she called. 'The water is coming out all brown.'

Harry ran into the kitchen. He looked at the water. 'Where does the town's water come from?' he asked.

'About eight kilometres away, up the mountain,' said Rachel.

'We have to go there, now,' Harry said. 'Get the children.'

♦

They drove fast up the mountain road. The sleepy children were in the back of the car. 'Here we are,' said Rachel, and stopped the car.

Harry got out. He and Rachel went over to the water. It was all brown. Harry walked round. 'There's gas all round here,' he said.

They drove quickly back to town. It was midnight. Harry hit the door of Paul's hotel room. When he opened the door, Harry went inside.

'What's happening?' said Paul.

'Look,' said Harry. He turned on the water in Paul's bathroom. An hour later, all the scientists were back in their office hard at work.

'The earthquakes are stronger now,' Harry said early the next morning. '2.3 or 2.4 every time.'

'There's a lot of gas too,' Stan said.

'This mountain is ready to explode,' said Nancy.

Paul Dreyfus put down the phone. 'More police are coming,' he said. 'They'll be here by midnight.'

Stan called over to Harry, 'How much time do you think we've got?'

'I don't know,' Harry said. He looked at Dreyfus.

Dreyfus said, 'Ask Mayor Wando to tell the people of the town to be ready to leave.'

◆

At six in the evening, Rachel, Harry and the two children were in the café. Rachel was on the phone. 'Ruth,' she said for the fifth time, 'you must come down to the town now. It's dangerous. We're going to leave. You must come with us.'

'I'm not leaving,' Ruth said. She looked out of the window at the trees and the lake. 'This is my home.' She put down the phone.

Rachel went to the school. The townspeople waited there for her.

'You must leave your homes,' she said. 'Some of you will find it hard, but you must.'

Elliot Blair got up and left the room. Les Worrell watched him go. He could do nothing.

'Must we wait, Rachel?' a young woman asked. 'Can we leave now?'

'Yes,' Rachel said. 'Leave now.'

Ten or twelve other people stood up and left the room.

*Out on the street they looked up at the mountain.*

Harry Dalton got up to speak. 'We're asking you to be ready to leave,' he said, 'because we don't want to see anything bad happen. But we don't want you to be afraid.'

But then the school building moved. People jumped up out of their chairs. Somebody screamed. Everybody ran for the doors.

Out on the street they looked up at the mountain. The volcano threw ash and smoke and gases up into the sky. People ran through the town. Children screamed for their mothers and fathers.

At Rachel's house Graham saw the mountain through the window. 'Lauren!' he called. 'Let's go! We're leaving now!'

At the hotel Dreyfus looked at the equipment. 'The lava is starting to move,' he said.

'Don't look at the equipment,' Nancy said. 'Look out of the window.'

The smoke from the peak was dark. It was lava ash. 'Dante's Peak is going to be more dangerous than Mount St Helen's,' Paul said. 'And the explosion will come soon.'

## Chapter 10   A Letter from Graham

Outside, Rachel and Harry looked at the mountain. 'You were right,' she said.

A building fell on to the school bus. 'I must go home. I must get the children,' Rachel said.

'Let's take my car,' said Harry. They ran over to his off-road car. They had to push through a lot of people.

There were earthquakes all the time now. Buildings fell, windows broke. The road broke open and a car drove into it.

Harry spoke on the radio. 'Paul, are you there?'

'Yes,' said Paul. 'We're at the hotel. We're taking the equipment and leaving. Where are you?'

'I'm with Rachel. We're going to get her children.'

'Harry,' said Paul, 'I'm sorry. You were right and I was wrong.'

'Forget it, Paul,' Harry said. 'See you soon!' He turned off the radio.

But when they came to Rachel's house, she screamed. 'My car!' she said. 'It's not here!'

She ran into the house. 'Here's a letter from Graham,' she cried. 'He says he wants to get Ruth! He's driving up the mountain!'

Harry fought through the other cars. He couldn't drive across the river by the road, because there were too many cars. The water in the river flowed strongly. 'We can do it in this car,' he said. He drove into the river. The water pulled at them, but Harry's car got through. Other cars began to follow, but were not as lucky. The water turned them over.

Behind them, the garage exploded in the town, and fires started.

♦

In the hotel Greg looked at his equipment. 'The lava is coming up,' he said. 'It's very near the ground now.'

Some people waited outside the hotel. 'Why are these people here?' asked Nancy.

'The helicopter's coming for them,' Paul said.

Now the people could hear the sound of the helicopter in the night sky. Hutcherson brought the helicopter down by the hotel. He opened the door and looked at all the people. 'Eleven people only,' he said. 'No more than eleven.'

Elliot Blair, Les Worrell and some others took out a lot of money. They paid Hutcherson, and smiled. 'We'll get out of here,' Les said to Blair.

In the hotel, Paul said, 'Why is Hutcherson flying out? It's too dangerous.'

He ran outside, but it was too late. The helicopter left the ground. 'They paid him fifteen thousand dollars each,' somebody said.

'Stop! Stop!' called Paul. 'There's too much ash. You can't fly in all that ash.' But nobody in the helicopter heard him.

He watched the helicopter. It flew over the town. With twelve people in it, it flew slowly. It was heavy. It flew into a lot of ash. The ash got inside the engine, and suddenly the engine stopped.

Harry drove the car past the last buildings of the town. Suddenly he stopped the car. The helicopter hit the mountain on their right, fell across the road in front of them, and exploded.

Harry spoke into his radio. 'A helicopter is down on Exeter Street. Send help.'

'OK, Harry,' said Stan. 'What are you doing? Where are you?'

'We're driving up the mountain,' Harry said. 'We must get Rachel's children.' He turned off the radio.

'Harry, listen to me,' Stan said. 'There's no time, Harry. Come back. The lava . . .' But there was no answer from the radio.

*Harry and Rachel drove up the road. Then the strong earthquake hit them too. Big rocks fell into the road behind them.*

## Chapter 11   River of Red

The lights were on in Ruth's house. Graham stopped the car in front of it. The children jumped out and ran to the house.

Ruth came out of the front door with Roughy. 'What are *you* doing here?' she asked.

'We came to get you and Roughy out,' they said.

'What?' she said.

'Get in the car,' Graham said. He pulled her hand.

A sudden strong earthquake moved the ground. Roughy ran into the trees. Lauren ran after her. 'Roughy! Roughy!' she called.

◆

Harry and Rachel drove up the road. 'Not far now,' Rachel said. Then the strong earthquake hit them too. Big rocks fell into the road behind them. Rachel looked at Harry. 'Now we can't come back down this road,' she said.

◆

In the dark trees Ruth and the children called for Roughy. Ruth got tired. She stopped calling. She heard the children. They were young. 'I must get them out of here,' she thought.

'Ruth, can you see Roughy?' said Lauren.

'No, I can't,' Ruth said. 'And it's too late now. We must go. Now.'

'But we can't leave her!'

The children looked at Ruth. She was different, stronger. 'I said now,' she said.

◆

Harry stopped the car outside Ruth's house. They saw Rachel's car there. Rachel jumped out and ran into the house. 'Ruth! Graham! Lauren!' she called. There was no answer.

'Where are they?' said Harry. 'The lights are on.'

Then Ruth and the children came out of the trees. Rachel ran over to them. She put her arms round them. 'Where were you?' she said. 'I'm angry and happy at the same time.'

'I'm sorry, Mom,' said Graham. 'We had to get Ruth.'

'There's no time for this now,' said Ruth. 'Get the children into the car and get out of here.'

'We can't do that,' Harry said. 'There are rocks all over the road behind us. And you're coming with us.'

'OK,' said Ruth. 'Give me five minutes. I must get some things.'

◆

Harry spoke on the radio to the scientists at the hotel. 'Is anybody there?' he asked.

'Harry, where are you?' said Dreyfus.

'Up at the lake,' Harry said. 'We're OK, but there's no road for us to come back down the mountain.'

'Harry,' Paul said, 'this mountain is going to explode . . . and soon. I'll send a helicopter up to get you.'

'No, get out of there,' Harry said, 'before it's too late. Don't wait for us.' The radio started to die. 'Harry, can you hear me?' Paul said.

'Can you hear me?' He looked at the others. 'The radio's dead,' he said.

◆

Rachel and Ruth threw things in some bags. Ruth wanted to take everything. 'This is my home,' she said. 'All my things are here.'

Rachel wanted to cry: 'Let's go! Leave all that! Let's go!'

Up on the mountain above Ruth's house a river of red lava began to flow down the mountain. Fire suddenly caught on the trees. The river of lava left everything dead behind it.

*Then the lava broke the window and flowed into the house.*

The lava came to Ruth's house. It flowed round to the left and to the right. It flowed round to the front of the house. The cars stood there. Fire started to climb up the outside of the house.

Harry looked out of the back window of the house and saw the lava. Then the lava broke the window and flowed into the house. Fire ate chairs, tables, everything. Harry and Rachel pushed the children to the front door. Ruth followed with her bags.

Rachel screamed: 'Look! The cars!'

Red hot lava flowed under the cars. Lava flowed from the left and right into the lake. 'There's only the lake,' Harry said. 'Let's go!'

They ran down to the lake and jumped into Ruth's small boat. 'Now we'll be OK,' Graham said to Lauren.

Then they saw the fish. Hundreds of dead fish on the water.

Harry tried to start the boat's engine. He couldn't do it. Ruth said, 'I know this boat. I'll do it.' She started the boat and they moved out across the water.

They looked back at Ruth's house. There was fire everywhere. 'That was my home,' Ruth said. 'I always lived there.'

Everybody was very quiet. One of the cars exploded. 'Where's Roughy?' the children thought.

'This boat is slow,' Harry said, 'but it'll get us there.'

Then he heard a different noise. 'Where's that noise coming from?' he thought. 'Ah, yes, under the boat . . .' He looked down.

'Don't put your hands in the water,' he said.

'Why?' Rachel asked.

'The water's acid.'

Graham said, 'The acid is eating into the boat. Will it get us there?'

Harry didn't answer.


## Chapter 12   Line of Fire

Soon the acid ate through, into the boat. Acid water began to flow into the boat. 'Put your feet up, out of the water,' Harry said. 'We only have a hundred metres to go.'

Then he heard a different noise, much worse. 'The engine is stopping,' he said. He tried not to be afraid. 'The acid ate into the engine. There are only thirty or forty metres to go. Perhaps we'll get there.'

The boat moved slowly on. Thirty metres, twenty, ten . . . 'Graham, give me your coat,' Harry said.

He put the coat round his hand and used his hand to move the boat in the water. But the acid quickly ate  through the coat, and then the boat stopped. 'Only five metres to go,' Harry said. 'That tree is near – perhaps I can get to it and pull us in.' He tried, but he couldn't. He tried again.

'Forget it, Harry,' Ruth said. 'You can't do it.' She looked down at the water. 'I can stand here,' she said.

Harry turned round. 'Ruth, no!' he said.

But Ruth started to get out of the boat. Harry moved to stop her but she pulled away. She stood in the water and pushed the boat. The acid ate at her legs.

Rachel, Harry and the children jumped out of the boat, on to the ground. Then Ruth screamed. She tried to walk to them, but she fell on the ground. 'Don't come near,' she said. 'The acid . . .'

They sat and watched her die. 'Oh, Ruth,' Rachel cried. 'I love you.' Ruth smiled up at her.

'My son didn't know you, Rachel,' she said. 'You're good. I want you to be happy.' She looked at Harry and closed her eyes. She never spoke again. Rachel and the children cried.

◆

The sky was thick with ash and gases. Harry, Rachel and the children walked down the mountain. They were tired, and wet with dirty, black rain. Now they could see the town. Suddenly they heard a big noise to their right. 'What's that?' asked Rachel.

'Water, trees, rocks, buildings – all coming fast down the mountain,' Harry said. 'They're going to hit the river – the river through Dante's Peak.'

In Dante's Peak Paul Dreyfus and the other scientists were at the radio. 'Harry, can you hear me?' said Paul. 'Harry, we must leave now. It's too dangerous for us to stay. Sorry.'

They put their equipment in their cars. Dreyfus drove the car with all the equipment, and the others all went in the first car. The first car got across the river. Dreyfus, in the second car, looked up. The river was now much bigger than usual. It was flowing fast, and there were rocks and trees in it. It flowed on to the road and carried his car away. He only had time for one scream before he died.

Harry found an old car. Luckily, the engine started. They got into it and began to drive. Small rocks hit the car; large rocks hit the ground near them. Harry thought of Marianne. 'Not again, please,' he thought.

Round the corner they came to a river of lava. 'Can we drive across that?' Rachel asked.

'I don't know,' Harry said. 'But we must try.' He drove as fast as he could at the lava. A line of fire followed them across the lava.

Suddenly Lauren cried, 'Look! There's Roughy!'

Roughy waited for them across the lava. 'How did she get here?' Harry said.

'Look!' Graham said. 'More lava is coming up behind Roughy.'

'We can't stop,' Harry said. 'Roughy will have one try only.'

They drove along slowly. Roughy ran up to the car. Rachel opened her door. 'Come on, Roughy!' she called. 'Jump!'

The children screamed, 'You can do it, Roughy!'

Roughy jumped. Rachel caught her and pulled her into the car. The children threw their arms round the dog. They laughed. Harry and Rachel laughed too.

## Chapter 13   The Old Mine

They drove into Dante's Peak, but it was not the same town. 'Fire and earthquakes did their worst here,' Rachel said sadly. 'It was a beautiful town. I was happy to be the mayor.'

They came to the river. 'We can't get across that,' Harry said, 'and there's more lava coming.'

'What can we do?' Rachel asked.

'We must get under the ground,' Harry said. 'But how?'

Graham looked at him. 'I know,' he said. 'The mine.'

♦

*The children screamed, 'You can do it, Roughy!'*

Nancy, Terry, Stan and Greg climbed out of the car and turned to look back at the mountain. A *big* earthquake hit, and the peak of the volcano exploded. New, red-hot lava flowed down the mountain. 'Goodbye, Harry,' said Terry angrily. Nancy started to cry.

In the car Harry, Rachel and the children heard the sounds of the explosion. They were near the mine. They looked up at the mountain. Something dark moved down the mountain very, very fast.

'Hot ash and rocks,' Harry said. 'When it hits us, we're dead. No mistakes, now! I have only one try.'

The car engine screamed. Harry drove fast into the mouth of the mine. Behind them, rocks fell thick and fast. The lava couldn't get in . . . but they couldn't get out.

'Is everybody OK?' asked Harry, when the car stopped. He kicked out the front window of the car and helped the others out.

'Graham,' Harry said, 'can we get out of the mine?'

'No we can't,' Graham said. 'I know these mines. We must wait. But it's OK. My friends and I left some food and drink here. Come with me.'

They followed Graham down into the mine. He showed them the food and drink. There were lights there too. They sat and ate some food.

Earthquakes moved the ground. Rocks fell in the mine. 'We're going to die here,' Lauren cried.

'The radio!' Harry suddenly remembered. 'I left the radio in the car. I must go back and get it.'

'No, I'll go,' Graham said.

'No, you stay,' Harry said.

'We're going to die,' cried Lauren.

'No, we're not,' Harry said. 'Hey, I know. When we get out,

we'll all go to the sea and catch fish. I don't usually take holidays, but with you it will be good. OK? We'll do that?'

Rachel looked at Harry and smiled. 'Yeah,' she said. 'We'll do that together. We'll be a family.'

'OK,' said Harry. 'But now I must go.'

He walked back through the mine. Suddenly he heard a sound above him. He ran for the car. Behind him, rocks fell. He couldn't go back. More and more rocks fell. He was near the car when a rock hit his left arm and broke it. Other rocks hit his head and his legs.

He climbed inside the car, found the radio and turned it on. 'Help,' he said. 'Please send help.'

Two days later, the earthquakes stopped. The volcano went quiet. A big helicopter came down outside the mine. Inside, when they pulled away hundreds of rocks, they found Harry first, with the radio in his hands.

He stood by the helicopter, and a doctor looked at his arm. Then the men brought Rachel and the children out of the mine. Harry walked over to them.

'Wait!' the doctor said. 'Your arm . . .'

But Harry had his arms round Rachel. The children ran up and he took them in his arms too. Nobody said a word – they were too happy.

# ACTIVITIES

**Chapters 1–3**

*Before you read*

1  Look at the Word List at the back of the book.
   a  Find the new words in your dictionary.
   b  Find four things that come out of volcanoes.
2  Read the Introduction to the book and answer these questions.
   a  Does Harry think the old volcano is dangerous?
   b  What is Harry's problem with his boss?
   c  Did the story in *Dante's Peak* really happen?
3  Look at the map before Chapter 1 and answer these questions.
   a  Where are the Cascade Mountains?
   b  What do you know about one of the mountains?
   c  What happens when a volcano explodes?

*While you read*

4  Write the names of people from the story. Who:
   a  sees his girlfriend die when a South
      American volcano explodes                    .........................
   b  is the mayor of Dante's Peak?                .........................
   c  is the most important businessman in
      Dante's Peak?                                .........................
   d  writes about Dante's Peak in a newspaper?    .........................
   e  wants to make Dante's Peak a centre for
      winter holidays?                             .........................
   f  is Rachel Wando's son?                       .........................

*After you read*

5  How does Harry feel after:
   a  his girlfriend dies?
   b  Paul tells him about Dante's Peak in Washington?
   c  he sees the mayor for the first time?

**6** Why are these important to the story?

   **a** the newspaper story 'The Second Best Town in America'

   **b** Elliot Blair's plans for Dante's Peak

   **c** the two swimmers

## Chapters 4–6

*Before you read*

  **7** Look at the pictures in Chapters 4, 5 and 6 and discuss these questions.

   **a** Will the mayor want to help Harry or will she want to stop him. Why?

   **b** What or who is 'Sleeping, not dead' in Chapter 5?

   **c** Why do Harry and Terry go up in a helicopter?

*While you read*

  **8** <u>Underline</u> the right word in *italics*.

   **a** Harry's equipment found too much *hot water / acid* in the lake.

   **b** Lauren screamed when she saw two dead *animals / people* in the water.

   **c** Harry wants Paul to come to Dante's Peak with *money / a robot*.

   **d** 'The volcano is sleeping, not dead,' says *Sheriff Turner / Harry*.

   **e** The businessmen are happy because *Paul / Harry* doesn't want people to move out of the town.

   **f** In the helicopter, Harry and Terry's equipment shows gas in the mountain but it doesn't show the small *volcano / earthquake*.

*After you read*

  **9** Talk to another student. What do you know about:

   **a** Ruth and Rachel?

   **b** Paul's plan and Harry's plan for the people of Dante's Peak?

   **c** Harry's girlfriend, Marianne, and Rachel's husband?

 **10** How does Rachel feel differently about Harry now? Why?

## Chapters 7–9

*Before you read*

**11** Look at the pictures in Chapters 7, 8 and 9. What is happening in each picture?

**12** Which of these will change, do you think? How?

    **a** the number of earthquakes

    **b** Elliot Blair's money-making plans for Dante's Peak

    **c** the town's people

    **d** the volcano

*While you read*

**13** Put these words in the sentences.

    *ash   equipment   helicopter   lava   radio   robot*

    **a** The ........................ can go inside the volcano and find out about it.

    **b** The scientists in the office watch their ........................ and can see pictures from inside the volcano.

    **c** After Terry breaks his leg, Harry speaks to Hutcherson by ........................ .

    **d** Hutcherson brings the ........................ nearer to the volcano and pulls Harry and Terry up and away.

    **e** Harry is afraid because the ground is very warm from the hot ........................ .

    **f** Smoke and ........................ from the volcano begin to fill the sky.

*After you read*

**14** Who says these things? Why?

    **a** 'When a bird jumps on to the ground, we'll know it.'

    **b** 'Come back now. Earthquake!'

    **c** 'Only fifteen more metres! Down! Down!'

    **d** 'I want to put eighteen million dollars into Dante's Peak, not Pompeii.'

43

**15** Work with another student. Have this conversation.

  *Student A:*   You are Harry. You want everybody to leave the town. Tell Les Worrell about the two swimmers, the dead fish, Terry and the robot.

  *Student B:*   You are Les Worrell. You think Harry is wrong. Tell him and say why.

**16** Discuss: How does Paul feel about the future of the town before the water turns brown? How does he feel after that?


## Chapters 10–11

*Before you read*

**17** Look at the pictures in Chapters 10 and 11. What will happen to these people, do you think?

  **a**  Ruth and her dog Roughy      **c**  Graham and Lauren

  **b**  Rachel and Harry              **d**  Elliot Blair and Les Worrell

**18** Chapter 10 is 'A Letter from Graham.' Who does he write a letter to, do you think? Why?

*While you read*

**19** What happens first? What happens next? Write the numbers 1–8.

  **a**  Harry sees Hutcherson's helicopter when it hits the mountain. .....

  **b**  Rachel finds Graham's letter about Ruth. .....

  **c**  Harry, Rachel, Ruth and the children get into Ruth's boat. .....

  **d**  Rocks fall on the road behind Harry's car, so he and Rachel can't drive back down the mountain. .....

  **e**  Paul says to Harry, 'I'm sorry. You were right and I was wrong.' .....

  **f**  The acid in the lake starts eating into the boat. .....

  **g**  Elliot Blair and Les Worrell pay Hutcherson a lot of money to fly them away from Dante's Peak. .....

  **h**  A river of red hot lava flows into Ruth's house. .....

**20** Talk with another student about Graham, Rachel, Ruth, Lauren and Harry. Who or what is most important to each of them? What is most important to Blair, Worrell and Hutcherson?

**21** What problems do Harry, Rachel, the children and Ruth have from the rocks, fire, lava and acid?

## Chapters 12–13

*Before you read*

**22** Do you think the boat will get across the lake? Will everybody on the boat live?

**23** Look at the picture and the sentences under it on page 37 and answer these questions.

    **a** What do you see in the sky and on the ground?

    **b** What does 'You can do it, Roughy!' mean?

    **c** How do you think Lauren got into a car?

*While you read*

**24** Are these sentences right (✓) or wrong (✗)?

    **a** Rachel gets out of the boat and pushes it through the acid. .....

    **b** The acid in the lake kills Ruth, and Paul dies in the river. .....

    **c** Harry finds an old car and drives through the lava to Dante's Peak. .....

    **d** When the volcano explodes, Harry drives inside the mountain. .....

    **e** There is no food or drink inside the mountain. .....

*After you read*

**25** Which people in the story lose family or friends? How does that change them, do you think?

**26** In Chapter 3, Rachel was angry when she found Graham inside the mountain with his friends. What does she think about that place at the end of the story, do you think?

## Writing

**28** What does Karen Narlington write about Dante's Peak in her newspaper story 'The Second Best Town in America'? Write it.

**29** How do the families of the two swimmers feel about the mayor of Dante's Peak after the volcano, do you think? Write a letter from one of their parents to Mayor Rachel Wando.

**30** Write about Paul Dreyfus and Harry Dalton for the United States Volcano Office. What lessons can the scientists there learn from these two men's ideas about the volcano at Dante's Peak? Did Paul make mistakes? Did Harry?

**31** What do you know about the helicopter man, Hutcherson, and the businessmen Les Worrell and Elliot Blair? What is important to these men? Write about why you like or don't like them in the story.

**32** Write a conversation between Graham and Lauren the day after they come out of the mountain. What are they sad about and what are they happy about, do you think? What are their problems now? What do they think about their future and the future of Dante's Peak?

**33** Write Chapter 14. What will happen between Rachel and Harry after the story ends? Where will Rachel and her children live? What will happen to Dante's Peak? What will Harry do?

**34** You are Rachel. Write a letter to your old husband. Tell him about his mother, Ruth. What happened on the mountain and in the lake? How does Rachel feel about Ruth?

**35** Which do you think are more dangerous, earthquakes or volcanoes? Why? Write your ideas.

Answers for the Activities in this book are available from the Penguin Readers website. A free Activity Worksheet is also available from the website. Activity Worksheets are part of the Penguin Teacher Support Programme, which also includes Progress Tests and Graded Reader Guidelines. For more information, please visit: www.penguinreaders.com.

# WORD LIST *with example sentences*

**acid** (n) Be careful. The *acid* in that bottle is very strong. It can hurt your hand.

**ash** (n) After the fire, there was a lot of grey *ash* on the ground.

**business** (n) There are shops, restaurants, hotels and many other *businesses* in the town.

**earthquake** (n) When the *earthquake* started, we felt the ground moving.

**engine** (n) He got into the car and started the *engine*.

**equipment** (n) He put the computer, the radio and other *equipment* into his bag.

**explode** (v) The plane hit the ground and *exploded* into a ball of fire. People heard the *explosion* 5 kilometres away.

**flow** (v) Water *flows* down rivers to the sea.

**gas** (n) We get *gas* from under the ground, and we use it for cooking.

**helicopter** (n) The people on the boat got into the *helicopter*, and it flew away.

**lake** (n) We walked round the *lake* and then we swam in it.

**lava** (n) Red-hot *lava* flowed out of the volcano and down the mountain.

**mayor** (n) The *mayor* of New York spoke to the people of the city on TV.

**must** (v) We haven't got any food. We *must* buy some.

**peak** (n) We climbed up the mountain, all the way up to its *peak*.

**robot** (n) This *robot* can walk and talk and do small jobs. Who made it?

**rock** (n) A big *rock* broke way from the mountain and fell onto the road.

**scientist** (n) Albert Einstein was the most famous *scientist* in the world.

**scream** (v) When she saw it, she *screamed* loudly and ran away.

**volcano** (n) That mountain is a dead *volcano*.

## Pirates of the Caribbean
*The Curse of the Black Pearl*

Elizabeth lives on a Caribbean island, a very dangerous place. A young blacksmith is interested in her, but pirates are interested too. Where do the pirates come from and what do they want? Is there really a curse on their ship? And why can't they enjoy their gold?

## Moby Dick
*Herman Melville*

Moby Dick is the most dangerous whale in the oceans. Captain Ahab fought him and lost a leg. Now he hates Moby Dick. He wants to kill him. But can Captain Ahab and his men find the great white whale? A young sailor, Ishmael, tells the story of their exciting and dangerous trip.

## Jaws

Amity is a quiet town near New York. One night a woman goes for a swim in the sea. The next morning somebody finds her body on the beach. Brody is the Amity policeman. He thinks there's a killer shark out there. But the important people don't listen to him.

*There are hundreds of Penguin Readers to choose from – world classics, film adaptations, modern-day crime and adventure, short stories, biographies, American classics, non-fiction, plays ...*

For a complete list of all Penguin Readers titles, please contact your local Pearson Longman office or visit our website.

## Jumanji

Be careful when you throw the Jumanji dice! What will happen?
Nobody knows, but it will be dangerous. Two children find the
game and start to play. Jungle animals and a man with a gun come
out of the board. How can they stop them? They must finish the
game.

## A Christmas Carol
*Charles Dickens*

Scrooge is a cold, hard man. He loves money, and he doesn't like
people. He really doesn't like Christmas. But then some ghosts
visit him. They show him his past life, his life now, and a possible
future. Will Scrooge learn from the ghosts? Can he change?

## Kidnapped
*Robert Louis Stevenson*

After his parents die, young David Balfour goes to the house of his
uncle Ebenezer. But his uncle is a dangerous man. When he puts
David on a ship to America, a difficult and dangerous time begins.
But who is the stranger on the ship? Can he help David?

*There are hundreds of Penguin Readers to choose from – world classics,
film adaptations, modern-day crime and adventure, short stories,
biographies, American classics, non-fiction, plays ...*

For a complete list of all Penguin Readers titles, please contact your local
Pearson Longman office or visit our website.

**www.penguinreaders.com**

02033453000

# Longman Dictionaries

PEARSON
Longman

Express yourself with confidence!

*Longman has led the way in ELT dictionaries since 1935.
We constantly talk to students and teachers around the
world to find out what they need from a learner's dictionary.*

### *Why choose a Longman dictionary?*

### Easy to understand

Longman invented the Defining Vocabulary – 2000 of the most
common words which are used to write the definitions in our
dictionaries. So Longman definitions are always clear and easy
to understand.

### Real, natural English

All Longman dictionaries contain natural examples taken from
real-life that help explain the meaning of a word and show you
how to use it in context.

### Avoid common mistakes

Longman dictionaries are written specially for learners, and we
make sure that you get all the help you need to avoid common
mistakes. We analyse typical learners' mistakes and include
notes on how to avoid them.

### Innovative CD-ROMs

Longman are leaders in dictionary CD-ROM innovation. Did
you know that a dictionary CD-ROM includes features to help
improve your pronunciation, help you practice for exams and
improve your writing skills?

**For details of all Longman dictionaries, and to choose
the one that's right for you, visit our website:**

**www.longman.com/dictionaries**